Zoe th

The Rescue Mission

Lucia Matuonto - author, illustrator

Luma Studio

This book is dedicated to my mother, who took me many times to the library; to my daughter, to whom I used to read bedtime stories; to my husband, who is always encouraging me to pursue my dreams; to my patients, who taught me hope and perseverance, and to Celina, who loves reading my books.

Lucia Matuonto

2020

"I guess there are never enough books."
— John Steinbeck

1. Summer

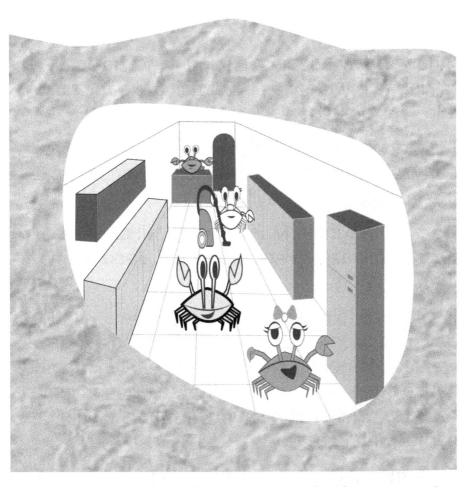

Hurrah, what a joy! Our long-awaited summer is coming. Our house is getting warmer and I can already hear the beautiful song of the cicadas in the evenings.

We're counting down the days until we can go sliding on the fine sand and throw ourselves into the endless turquoise ocean.

We crabs love to feel the warmth of the sun and the touch of salt water cooling our shells. Of course, too much heat makes us feel unwell and that's why we like to spend the day playing in the sea.

I have many hobbies: exploring new places, talking to my friends and dancing are my absolute favorites.

I'm planning to run, dance and jump freely very early in the morning, because at 6 am, most of the human feet are still sleeping quietly.

During the winter, Mom used to tell us stories to help us fall asleep and we would sleep for more than 12 hours.

It's so nice to sleep under the blankets without having a fixed time to wake up. On colder days, we used to get up just in time to eat lunch or because Juan woke up and started talking uninterruptedly, while Paco spent the whole day in the corner writing poetry.

One morning, Juan pulled me out of my deep sleep to complain.

"Sis, I think Paco is becoming an adult. He doesn't even want to play with me anymore."

"Leave him alone, Juan, at least he is quiet," I replied without opening my eyes.

"But I have no one to play with."

"So, Juan, keep on sleeping, rest for the summer!"

Teens! I think that adolescence is a very strange phase. Sometimes, Paco frowns even if nothing has happened, but soon after he turns happy again and starts telling jokes. Does anyone understand this?

Juan, despite being younger, already has a different voice, but still remains silly.

I think of Mom's wise words:

"Everything changes, children. We are part of nature and we follow this continuous cycle of transformations from the time we're born."

2. Nature

Speaking of changes, we realized that last winter was not as cold as previous winters. We often managed to stretch our eyes outside the house and talk to Sofia and Ned.

Ned was often very pensive, lost in his thoughts, and told us that the temperature of our planet is rising.

"Don't worry Ned, it's a cycle," I repeated Mom's words.

"Unfortunately not, Zoe. Studies show that humans are causing this change. If they don't modify their behavior, many species will soon be extinct."

"What do you mean? What kind of behavior?" Paco asked, startled.

"Humans produce tons of garbage daily and among them are plastics, which last for hundreds of years in the environment."

I felt a strong pounding in my chest and remembered the plastic bottles we'd seen floating in the ocean coming towards our beach.

"This is a photo of our planet from 20 years ago and this is a current photo." Ned stretched out his paws showing us the two satellite images.

We looked closely to compare the photos. We saw huge holes in the forests and an immense number of houses built where before there were only trees. I saw that the amount of green had decreased a lot and I started worrying about the animals that used to live there.

"Zoe, all this pollution raises the temperature of the land and the seas, increasing the chances of having large, powerful and destructive hurricanes." We looked in awe at the graphs full of curves, which we couldn't quite understand.

"I'm scared," said Sofia, "I haven't even laid my eggs yet and I'm already thinking about what will happen to my babies in the future."

"It's true, the last hurricane season was very intense," agreed Juan, remembering the intense noise of the wind. Ned and Sofia had to help us several times as we were buried for several days. Huge dunes formed over our house and our two friends had to use shovels to clear our exit.

During those days, our beach looked like the Sahara Desert with blue skies, very white sands and completely empty.

"And what can we do to change this worrisome trend, Ned?"

"We can't do anything, Zoe. Humans need to be aware of the environment, use cleaner energy and reduce waste."

"Clean energy?" asked Sofia, shaking her rattle.

"Yes, they can generate energy through the wind, the sun and even the waves of the sea."

"So, we have to recruit as many animals as possible to raise awareness of this!" I stated, triumphantly.

"But how do we do that?" Asked Paco.

"Zoe, you always have good ideas, but in this case we cannot do anything because humans don't understand our language and, even if they did, they wouldn't listen to us."

"Ned, you told me that men understand dogs and vice versa. Maybe we can become friends with some dogs and they can help us with this project?"

"I don't know, Zoe, dogs are unpredictable!" said Sofia. "One day one of them caught me and shook me like I was a rope. I only escaped because the owner shouted "snaaaaaake" and the dog released me."

"What a scare!" I agreed, imagining the scene.

"It's always like that. Even though I have a name, humans still call me 'snake'."

"They should read the necklace around your neck," Ned said, disappointed as I amused myself. Ned takes everything very seriously.

"Let's come up with a better plan then, but we cannot give up helping future generations," I proclaimed.

3. Paco

Mom organized a picnic for tomorrow to celebrate the new season and Jenny, Ned's mom, has been busy preparing various snacks and desserts for this important occasion.

Since Jenny came to live here on our beach, Mom started spending time with her and is much happier, because she finally has a good friend to share moments like this with.

"Good morning, friends! Tomorrow is a very special day as our long-awaited summer will begin. To celebrate, we'll have a picnic in the park together. We'll meet on the shore at nine in the morning so we can walk to the park all together," Mom announces on the loudspeaker.

"Perfect," agrees Sofia through the stereo system. Jenny follows the announcement with the menu planned for the next day.

I am relaxing in the hammock and making plans for tomorrow when little, silent steps come stealthily towards me.

"Zoe, I need to talk to you," whispers Paco, while looking carefully in all directions to be sure the others can't hear him.

When Paco wants to talk to me, I already know that there's a problem, or even two. It could either be something that recently happened or something that will hit us in the head at any moment as fast as a lightning bolt.

"What happened?" I jump out of the hammock and start thinking of all possible worst-case scenarios and potential solutions.

"I need your help, little sister," he says, humbly.

Hmmm, even with all my imagination I couldn't predict this. The issue must be dead serious.

Why?

Because:

Paco is never humble.

Paco never whispers.

Paco never stays silent for so long.

"You need my help?" I almost fall to the floor in my surprise.

"Yes, Zoe, because you've grown up now."

Of course! I'm already two years old. But he still doesn't let me lead our expeditions on the beach.

"What do you need, brother?" I am flattered and worried at the same time.

"It's just that I...I like Suzy," announces Paco, timidly.

"Wow, tell me something I don't know! Honey, the whole beach knows you like her."

"Okay, but she still doesn't know."

"So, is that it? Don't worry, I will tell her."

"No sister, I want to tell her myself. The only problem is that I still don't have the courage and I can't figure out the right moment."

"It's easy Paco, just give her flowers. Girls love flowers."

"I'm embarrassed."

"Then ask Juan to deliver the flowers and write her a nice card."

"No way, sister. In fact, I want you to invite Suzy to the picnic tomorrow so I can get close to her."

"Fine. I'll ask Sofia to slip an invitation into her house. Is there anything else I can do for you?"

"Just that, Zoe. Thanks, little sister!"

Paco and Juan are very close, but when Paco wants to talk about something important, he always looks for me.

Suzy is our neighbor and she's the princess of the entire beach. She's popular and very friendly. Suzy became fashionable last summer and always wears a stylish hat that she made herself. We're not very close friends, but, who knows, maybe she'll accept going out with us to celebrate the first day of summer.

4. Picnic

At 9 o'clock sharp we are all gathered on the shore. A flock of pelicans lands beside us and it looks like they want to take part in the banquet. Thankfully, pelicans prefer to eat fish, otherwise their picnic would start at this very moment with us on the menu!

The day is cool and cloudy, and Mom is worried about the possibility of heavy rains, which are typical of summer. According to Ned, we'll see all kind of climatic variations throughout the day.

"It says it's cloudy now, but it might be sunny in the next few hours," he says, reading the news.

"I can see it's cloudy without reading the news, Ned," Juan says in a mocking tone.

"This other website says it could rain at any time," reads Ned, confused.

"Don't believe all those predictions. We're better off watching the birds, as they fly lower when it rains," comments Juan, with the attitude of an expert.

"Really, in which book or scientific paper did you read that, Juan?"

"No, Ned, I've been watching the birds since I was born," says Juan proudly.

He then turns to me and asks, "Why is Paco so quiet?"

"I have no idea," I reply dismissively.

"Children, let's make a single file line and hold each other's claws. Zoe, stay with me because I don't want you to disappear again," says Mum, holding my little claw.

Standing in line, we start the warm-up ritual. We get up and open our claws several times in the air as if we could touch the sky, bend our knees sideways and bulge our eyes to the side. At my signal, we start running all together towards the park in disarray.

A few seconds later, we hear a call in the distance and spot Suzy running towards us, trying to catch up.

"Hi Zoe," she says breathlessly, "thank you for inviting me. I just saw the invitation now and I had little time to get ready."

What is she talking about? She looks perfect!

"I'm glad you came," I say, letting go of Mom's claw and holding Suzy's. From the corner of my eye I see Paco smiling at me.

"Zoe, I always wanted to be your friend," she shouts as we run. This declaration makes me very happy.

We run for about ten minutes, zigzagging to dodge human feet and sometimes falling abruptly into unexpected holes in the sand. Thirsty and sweaty, we arrive at a place with several statues, benches, a lake full of ducks and dozens of blossomed trees.

We choose a corner near the lake, settle down and unpack our snacks. A pleasant breeze sways the branches of the trees and little flowers float in the air above us.

"How about we play hide and seek over there?" Juan asks the group.

"Don't get hurt," Mom says.

"I knooooooow, Mom," growls Juan, climbing on a bench.

"I prefer to help with setting the table," replies Paco, standing next to Suzy.

"I'm staying here with my friends," I tell Juan.

"Playing alone isn't fun," says Juan, giving up.

As we prepare the table, we hear a human cry and quickly hide behind the trees. I decide to stretch my eyes out and an unexpected scene catches me by surprise. Molly, the girl I met on the island, who used to be a sloth is crying on the lawn in the park.

5. Revelation

"Molly?" I run towards her.

"Zoeeeeee! I can't believe it!" Molly says, picking me up.

"Molly, you and your dad disappeared. We were so worried."

"I am so glad I found you!" exclaims the girl with bright, blue eyes and a charming smile.
"I've been looking for you for days, picking into almost every hole on that huge beach."

"Molly, when did you come back from Australia? Did you find my father?" asks Ned, stuttering.

"I'm sorry Ned," says the girl with tears in her eyes. "My father was captured by the men who arrived on the island and I only managed to escape because I hid at the top of a tree."

"I'm so sorry!"

"I know Zoe, they took him on the boat and I spent days trying to get off the island. Luckily, a catamaran passed by and the crew heard my calls for help."

"And now, sweetie, what are you going to do?" Sofia asks, empathetically.

Molly bends down and starts to move her lips slowly. "I have to rescue my father," she sighs, "I need your help."

"The only way to get there quickly is by plane," says Ned, looking at my face, already expecting my reaction.

"Ned, you know I'll never get on a plane in my life. I'm scared of heights!" I reply, crossing my arms and stamping my feet on the floor.

"We can go by ship," says Molly.

"On a freighter?" Ned asks, already calculating the route.

"No, Ned, on a cruise ship. There is a ship that goes straight to Sydney, where my father is being kept."

"But, how do we get on a ship?" I ask, not understanding the plan.

"I can dress up as an adult and carry you in a bag. I have the address of the clinic and I believe that Sofia will be able to slither under the door and open it from the inside."

"I like your plan, Molly. I would love to finally explore a different place," Sofia states cheerfully.

"Sorry, but I'm not going. Imagine me on a ship!"

"Zoe, we need you," Molly says, looking at me deeply into the eyes.

I feel that now is the time to talk about my feelings and fears. These are my best friends and they should know why I am so afraid.

I take a step forward without knowing how to explain it and, finally, I let it all out at once.
"I...I lost my dad because of a fishing boat."

I look them in the eyes, one by one, as I watch their reactions.

"We were playing in the sea when a fishing net captured us. We were launched into the air towards a huge boat. Dad tried to cut the net but couldn't. I remember that I was taken out of the net and thrown back into the sea because I was still very small."

"And your father?" Molly asks.

"The fishermen took him, forever."

"Oh Zoe, I'm so sorry, I didn't know," says Molly, comforting me while Ned offers me a tissue.

"I'm sorry, sweetie," says Sofia. "Poor thing, you kept this burden for so long."

"Mom managed to rescue me with the help of a fish and I was able to survive, despite drinking a lot of seawater and having to stay in bed for weeks."

My friends look at me without knowing what to say.

"That's why I'm so afraid of heights and big boats."

"It was very sad to lose our father," adds Paco, sitting next to Suzy, while Juan lowers his head and walks away slowly.

"Zoe, I understand your pain, but a passenger ship is not like a fishing vessel. On a cruise, people have a lot of comfort and food. We will travel like VIP's! It'll be like a luxurious vacation," says Molly, trying her best to convince me.

"On a cruise, humans dance and have fun all the time," Ned shows us some pictures in a travel magazine.

"It's true! And we'll be locked in a fancy cabin. I won't let anything happen to you," Molly promises.

"I'll have to think about it, Molly. This is a very difficult decision for me, and anyway, I need to talk to Mom. I'm sure she won't like this idea one bit."

A tender voice whispers from behind the trees.

"Zoe, my dear daughter," says Mom from the corner from which she was watching us, "your father was a very good crab and he was always willing to do anything to help other people."

"He was the best dad in the world," murmurs Paco.

"Daughter, you have to make this decision alone. It's time for you to face your fears and challenges. After all, I will not always be here to protect you."

"According to elaborate statistics and the theory of chaos, our plan has a 50 percent chance of working out," Ned says while tapping frantically on the scientific, graphic calculator he holds in his paws.

Mom looks at me and says, fondly, "And who knows, daughter, with your smarts you could really help free Molly's father and all the other animals."

I keep quiet for a few seconds and run through my entire, short life. It wasn't fun to lose my claw but, after that, I have to admit that I became much braver.

My right claw has grown a little, but it's not like it used to be. However, that doesn't stop me from doing all kinds of things, like helping others. Just because I'm different doesn't mean that I have to feel inferior to other animals.

I see the sad expression in Molly's eyes and wonder what she must be feeling right now.
Molly was forced to live in the body of an animal and is now alone, far away from her father.

I really want to help Molly. But what about my fears?

Mom always says that being afraid is normal and it's important for us to overcome them and learn to survive.

According to Ned, hormones cause us to run away or fight back. I do prefer to run away whenever I can, because I'm small and any hit I make would not even scare a fly.

I stare at those friendly faces who look at me with compassion. With difficulty, I climb onto a rock, stretch my arms out and announce loudly, "Yes Molly, let's rescue your father!"
The small crowd gives me a standing ovation. Then we start eating.

6. Plan

The plan to get on the ship seemed very easy when Molly and Ned showed it to us on paper, but I'm changing my mind now that I see Molly's transformation: a 14-year-old girl dressed as a full-grown adult.

Molly is arriving at the beach, walking with difficulty and holding a bag made of palm tree leaves. The blue high-heeled shoes and yellow dress were donated by a used clothing store.

To complete the look, Molly is wearing a red, feather hat, which was found in a trash can by Paco, and purple, pearl earrings provided by Mom.

"These pearls are rare," says Mom, proud to help with the details, "an oyster must have forgotten them here."

Molly's huge, blue eyes widen, she tosses her long, black hair forward and stares at us for approval.

I don't really know if I should laugh or cry in front of the unexpected theatrical scene. Molly's performance as an adult is terrible and the fear of being caught at the ship's entrance is now greater than my fear of getting on it.

"So, guys, what do you think?" Molly asks from inside the dress that is twice her size.

Sofia is the first to respond, "Molly, you look beautiful, dear! You look like a model on the catwalk."

My brothers look at Sofia and start laughing while Ned promptly downloads videos of fashion shows.

"Look at this video, Molly, so you can learn how to walk better in high heels."

"We don't have time for this, Ned, the ship leaves tomorrow. Besides, right now I'm walking on sand, but it will be much easier when I'm on solid ground," Molly justifies as she looks at herself in the reflection of the sea.

"Molly, I think you need to wear lipstick," I say as I look for help in Ned's bag.

"Zoe, just give up. This bag is not giving me anything. I'm only using it because it looks cool."

"Cool?" Juan asks in a mocking tone.

"Juan, this is no time to joke, we're talking seriously here," says Paco, offering Suzy a flower.

"I knoooooow, Paco," says Juan.

"What if we stop at a makeup store on the way?"

"Good idea Zoe, but we don't know where to find such a store and we don't have time to look for one either. Just leave it to me. I know how to get on the ship without security realizing that I'm traveling without my parents," says Molly.

Ned starts talking about the plan, detailing what our next steps would be, from leaving the beach until we can relax safely inside the cabin. Ned manages to access the ship's blueprints and finds that some cabins are empty, so that we can get inside one of them and occupy it as if we are real passengers.

"What if we can't get a cabin?" Sofia asks frightened.

"We have to make it; failure is not an option," says Molly, talking like a fearless leader.

"The most important thing is for the three of us to stay in the bag without moving and making any noises. The rest is up to Molly," says Ned.

7. Boarding

On the day of the departure, we quickly say goodbye to avoid any sadness or weeping. Mom hugs me and wishes us 'good luck' as tears form in her eyes.

This time it is different! This is the first time I am leaving the beach on my own, willingly, and with Mom's approval, too.

Ned says goodbye to his mother and sister, Mia, promising them that everything will work out. Suzy hugs me warmly and wishes me luck. I am proud that I made this decision on my own, but, on the other hand, I am still uncertain of the possible outcomes of such a challenging mission.

We arrive at the harbor, all squeezed into Molly's bag. The sound of voices and music deafens us; it feels like we are at a party.
Molly has been walking in circles for a while and we're already travel-sick, even before boarding the ship.

Molly suddenly stops and speaks to us in a soft voice, "Girls and boy, it's time for action!"
As soon as Molly alerts us, she lurches and it feels like we're going to fall to the ground.

Soon after, we hear the sympathetic voice of a lady very close to us. "Poor thing, are you okay?" she asks as Molly pushes us back in the bag.

"I'm in pain, I think I sprained my ankle," Molly says, sobbing. "Could I hold onto you, please?" Molly asks as she hobbles.

"Of course, dear," agrees the lady. The sound of the security conveyor belt is getting closer and closer and my heart is beating faster and faster.

"Thank you so much, my name is Molly."

"I'm Rose, very pleased to meet you," says the lady with a big smile.

"Passports, please," the ship's agent asks firmly.

Molly lets go of Mrs. Rose's hand, puts the bag that carries us on the conveyor belt and hands over her passport, while talking to Mrs. Rose over-excitedly to cover her fear.
"Good thing we're traveling together," says Molly loudly as Mrs. Rose heads for the other belt.

"Miss, what's in these boxes?" asks another voice as gloved hands pull us out of the bag.

"They are gifts for my friends," Molly replies as we stand motionless, holding our breath.
Each one of us is in our own transparent box disguised as children's toys.

The human stares me right in the eyes, shakes me vigorously, passes a metal detector next to my face and throws me back on the belt.

Ned and Sofia go through the same process and are thrown on top of me. I was worried about the ship, but I start thinking that after having gone through all of this, cruising on the ship will be a piece of cake.

"All is fine, you can go with your aunt," says the human as Molly puts us hastily back into the bag.

Molly approaches Mrs. Rose gives her a hug and runs away with a map of the ship in her hands. Now I feel like I'm on a roller coaster. We enter a cabin at the end of the corridor and are finally taken out of the gift boxes.

"Yay! We did it!" I scream happily and a little incredulously.

"I was running out of air," says Sofia, sweating profusely.

"Did you know that we rabbits can survive for up to 15 minutes without breathing?" says Ned.

"So, Molly, let's put Ned back in that toy box," I say, laughing as Ned glares at me.

"Sorry Ned, it was just a joke. I won't do it again." Our plan is working!

8. On the high seas

First day at sea.

"Guys, we're going to be in this cabin for 30 days," Molly says, looking disappointed.

"I love this place, it's huge!" I state while settling in a corner of the cabin.

"Huge? Zoe, it's claustrophobic!" Molly replies.

"What does "claustrophobic" mean?" asks Ned.

"I can't believe you don't know, my dear, you always know everything!" exclaims Sofia.

"I just know that phobia means fear," he replies, without being able to check it in his books.

"Ned is correct," says Molly, "claustrophobia is fear of closed and small places. It's quite common among human beings."

"Good that we crabs don't have this claustro...thing, otherwise how could we live in that little hole we call home?"

We start laughing and sharing our experiences with the narrow spaces in our lives. Sofia says that when she was born, she had to make an enormous effort to reach the surface.

"Guys, I was born an athlete," says Sofia proudly, "I broke the egg with my teeth and got out of it easily. The hardest part was digging all day to get out of that deep hole."

"I can imagine your desperation, Sofia. I don't like closed places. Luckily, we have the porthole up there that we can leave open for some fresh air," says Molly, opening a small round window.

A pounding noise comes from the door and we hide under the bedsheets. Molly opens the door cautiously and a friendly voice introduces itself as Tony.
The boy says that he's the steward responsible for cleaning and organizing our cabin during our stay.
We hear Molly thanking the boy and telling him that there's no need to clean the cabin

every day, but Tony insists that this is his job and wishes her a pleasant trip.

"We have to be very careful. Tony will come here every day and you need to always be prepared to hide," says Molly.

"You can count on us," says Sofia, "I'll hide behind the curtain."

"I'll hide under the bed," says Ned.

"I'll hide in your shoe, Molly, I hope your feet don't stink," I joke.

Molly laughs, "My feet do not stink, but I don't know if that was also the case for the previous owner of the shoes."

We all laugh too and go to check out the bathroom and the cabinets. Finally, we watch the beautiful, calm sea through the small hatch.

"I'll sleep in the top bed and you guys in the bottom one," Molly says while climbing on the bunk bed.
"Great," says Ned, settling comfortably on the bottom bed.
"My plan is to only leave the room to get food every day because I want to limit the risk of

being discovered," says Molly, "but today, as it is the first day, we can take a small tour together to explore the ship."

"Yay!" we all reply, immediately jumping into the bag.

Molly walks barefoot along the ship's long corridors. Through holes in the bag, we see several human feet passing quickly and hear children's voices everywhere. Molly climbs several stairs until we reach the top deck of the ship.

We carefully stick our faces out of the bag and are amazed by what we see. It's like we are on a floating city with water parks, gyms, beauty salons, theaters and food courts. A lot of food courts.

"This looks like an amusement park, Dad would love this place," Molly exclaims excitedly.

We come across gigantic buffets with endless options of food, drinks and desserts. Molly tells us that passengers can eat anything they want, at any time they want, with no extra charge.
This is paradise!

After exploring all the restaurants and bumping into Mrs. Rose, Molly collects our generous lunch and heads back to our cabin. Here, we taste all the wonderful vegetarian delicacies she grabbed.

"If Paco and Juan were here, they would certainly be sick from stuffing their bellies to the limit," I say with my mouth full of seaweed from the Japanese restaurant.

We end up eating until we can't eat anymore. Sofia and Ned are so full that they doze off, while Molly and I keep talking.

"Molly, why did these humans take your father?" I ask.

"My father is a veterinarian and a researcher. I believe that these scientists need him to finish their experiments."

"But what are they trying to test or discover?"

"We don't know for sure, but my father said that they keep the animals in captivity and that they must be living in terrible conditions." "And why don't we just report them to the police?"

"Zoe, no one would believe or listen to a 14-year-old girl dressed as an adult, a rabbit without a tail, a snake called Sofia and a crab with a claw smaller than the other. First, we need to get Dad out of there so he can report them."

"So why did you insist that I come along? I'm small and I can't imagine how I could help."

"Zoe, you are very smart and I couldn't do it alone. I need your ideas and your support," she says, petting me. "Little Zoe, my plan ended when we got on the boat. In fact, I don't exactly know what we're going to do once we get off."

"How many people work in this laboratory?"

"I have no idea, but Sofia can infiltrate inside and give her cellphone to Dad. Ned will make the connection work and Dad will give us the details."

"And if everything works, what will we do with the animals?"

"Dad has contacts all over the world. I'm sure he will be able to find good people who will take care of them."

"Molly, you and your dad are very special."

9. Routine

15 days at sea.

Life on the ship has been very peaceful. We feel like babies who just eat, drink and sleep. The only catch is that we have to hide once a day when Tony comes to clean the cabin.

We spend the days being rocked by the waves and sometimes we get into the bag and go for a short tour with Molly. We have fun watching humans dance or play in the pool, and now I've gotten used to them a little more.

We had a scare once when Tony arrived early to clean the cabin. We were eating quietly and had suddenly to abandon our breakfast on the floor. Luckily, we managed to hide in a few seconds, but unfortunately, he threw our food in the garbage because he thought they were leftovers that Molly had forgotten on the floor.

I'm sure he now thinks that Molly is untidy and messy.

In the afternoon, we normally play cards and Molly tells stories about the time when she was turned into a sloth.

"Dad always loved animals and when those men approached us and told us that we could help save them, we were very happy. According to the men, a virus had emerged and would spread everywhere, infecting most of the animals."

"Those liars!" I say outraged.

"We collected the animals from their habitats and took them to the island. When Dad found out what the real reason was to keep them there, he tried to free them, but those men cast a spell on me and we were stuck on the island. Fortunately, with your help, I transformed back into a human and kept the power of being able to talk to animals."

That's it! Molly's power will help us raise human awareness for the protection of the environment.

20 days at sea.

We heard, over the speakers, that today there will be a Captain's party. Everyone should dress in white for the celebration dinner.

"Guys, I really want to go to this party. I met Mrs. Rose this week and she said she would pass by so that we go together. What do you think?"

"I think you should go, dear Molly. What do you think guys? We can make an outfit for her," says Sofia talking to me and Ned, while already planning the model of the dress.

We agree excitedly and start cutting some sheets, which turn into a beautiful white tunic that fits perfectly on Molly's body.

At 8 pm, Mrs. Rose knocks on the door and when Molly opens it, an elegant lady in a white embroidered dress storms into the cabin. We have only a second to get under the sheets and pillows. We are getting good at this.

"Molly, I can't take it anymore," she says, sitting down with all her weight over me.

"What happened? Let's go to dinner," says Molly, pulling Mrs. Rose's hand.

"The problem is my cabin mate. She snores all night and I can't sleep. Can I stay here for a couple of days until the crew finds me another place?"

"Mrs. Rose, why don't you talk to your cabin mate?"

"Of course, I did. But she says she can't do anything. I am exhausted, please let me stay."

 A silence hangs in the air as Rose takes the pillow, cries and clutches Ned's belly, who is hiding inside.

"Don't worry Mrs. Rose, you are most welcome," says Molly, persuading her to finally get up and out of the cabin. We recover from the shock and wait anxiously until eleven at night, after the party, when Molly, Mrs. Rose and a huge suitcase enter our little cabin.

10. D-Day

Mrs. Rose woke up early this morning and, without making a sound, dressed quietly and went out to have her breakfast. Last night, she told her story to Molly and we liked her right away.

Mrs. Rose has no family or home and practically lives on the road, spending months on long trips, visiting new places and making friends.

She never married and has no children, but she considers all the friends she meets as her children and nephews.

She does not have a home because she likes to travel and likes to constantly be surrounded by people. Therefore, she decided to share the cabin with an acquaintance from another trip.

Of course, since she moved into our cabin, our life got more complicated and we can only get out of hiding when neither Mrs. Rose nor Tony are in the room.

We cannot play our games all the time as we did before and we can no longer tour the ship with Molly, because Mrs. Rose is always with her. Mrs. Rose admitted that she's very happy that Molly had asked for help when boarding the ship, not knowing that everything had been carefully planned by us.

25 days at sea.

At lunchtime, they both went to the buffet and we were finally able to come out of our hiding places to stretch our bodies a little. Mrs. Rose had breakfast in the room and Molly had also stayed in the cabin to make sure that Mrs. Rose wouldn't discover us.

It's now already 2 pm and we still haven't eaten anything since Tony collected the leftovers on the floor yesterday. We're very hungry and don't understand why Molly is taking so long.

Sofia has a somewhat dangerous idea. "Zoe, I can crawl around the corner and up to the buffet. I'll slither under a table and pick up food crumbs from the floor."

"Sofia, the likelihood that someone will see you is very high, you'll have to crawl up several stairs," Ned warns.

"Look, I'm starving, but I can wait a little longer," I state with my hand on my belly.

"What if Molly is in danger? We need to know what's going on. Besides, I'm already training to release Mr. Jacobs," Sofia says, motivated.
"Okay, go, but take your cellphone, so you can tell us what is going on in real time. And put that towel over your body, so that no one sees a snake crawling across the ship," I advise.

Sofia goes under the door and slithers slowly down the hall until she reaches the stairs. She crawls through eight floors and is almost trampled when she reaches the food court.

Two small feet try to step on the towel, which suddenly comes alive and disentangles from underneath the feet, zigzagging away. The kid freezes, puzzled by what he sees, which looks like magic.

Sofia looks around quickly and sees Molly talking at a table with some people. Sofia crawls and snatches up a few pieces of food.

"Zoe and Ned, everything is under control," she whispers in the cellphone, almost choking with all the food in her mouth.

Mrs. Rose enters the cabin as soon as Sofia hangs up and, luckily, we're already hiding. A few minutes later Sofia comes through the cabin door and faces Mrs. Rose directly.

"SNAAAAAAAAKE! HEEEELP!" screams Mrs. Rose, climbing on Molly's bed like a rocket.

"HEEEEELP! GET ME OUT OF HERE!"

Sofia ducks under the bed, wraps us in her body and jumps out of the porthole, onto a string, while Tony invades the cabin with a fire extinguisher in his hands.

"Snake! Snake! There's a snake here in the cabin," Rose shouts from the top of the bed, covering every inch of her body with the blankets.

"A snake?" Tony asks, frowning.

"I saw a long green snake."

Tony searches everywhere with a flashlight.

"Mrs. Rose, there's no snake here."

Suddenly, Molly enters the cabin and is baffled by the scene.

"Molly, there's a snake in YOUR cabin!"

"Mrs. Rose, there are no snakes on ships," says Molly, taking Tony aside and whispering that Mrs. Rose sometimes hallucinates when she eats too much. "It must be some kind of self-defense reaction from her digestive system…"

Tony turns towards the cabin, struggles to take Mrs. Rose off the bed and convinces her to drink some water. "Don't worry, Mrs. Rose, I can get you a powerful antacid." She looks at him astonished, thinking that he lost his mind. How would an antacid help against snakes?

Ned calls Molly from outside the porthole until she rescues us and brings us back into the cabin. Finally! My jaw couldn't hold on anymore. I've been holding a rope that's hanging along the side of the ship with my mouth.

Sofia and Ned were holding on tight onto my little legs. A few more seconds and all of us would have made a big splash into the sea underneath.

"Guys, what did you do?" says Molly in shock, but relieved that Rose has left the cabin.

"Sofia went to get food. We were hungry, Molly," Ned says.

"You disappeared, Molly," says Sofia.

"We could have been discovered," I say, a bit disgruntled.

"I'm sorry, team, I did not forget you. Mrs. Rose and I ended up eating with two ladies. When we finished eating, Mrs. Rose invited them to come to our cabin."

"Seriously?" I ask incredulously.

"Yes. I told Mrs. Rose that I was going to sleep and suggested that they come another day. Imagine if they saw you!"

"Can you imagine Mrs. Rose and two other women talking inside this cabin?" I say, more relaxed and getting my sense of humor back.

"Women speak an average of 20,000 words a day," Ned says.

"Men also talk a lot," says Sofia, admiring her figure in the mirror.

"It's true," I chime in, "my brothers don't stop talking for a second."

"Then Mrs. Rose said she would go to the bathroom and be back," continues Molly, "I was waiting and since she didn't show up, I decided to come and bring you food," says Molly taking a squashed pizza out of the bag.

"Yeah, she was opening the suitcase when I entered. She saw me, screamed and the confusion started. I don't know how I didn't have a heart attack!" says Sofia.

"Sorry, my friends, I had no option but to stay a little longer and try to change her mind. Mrs. Rose offered to lend them some jewelry and wanted them to come and try it here."

"Mrs. Rose sometimes crosses the line", says Sofia, devouring the pizza.

11. The Arrival

30 days at sea.

Mrs. Rose and Molly spent the day talking animatedly. They are excited about the arrival and Mrs. Rose asked Molly about her parents.

"My dad is a veterinarian and I'm going to meet him. I can't wait."

"And where is your mother?"

"I never met my mother, my father adopted me when I was a little girl and since then we have always been together. This is the first time we have been apart."

We're taken by surprise with this revelation.

"And is your father in Australia on business?" Rose does not stop asking personal questions.

"He is, I mean, more or less. It's good that we're almost there," Molly says, dismissively.

Our ship passed close to the famous Opera House and is now stopped and anchoring. We are very curious and, at the same time, concerned about what's about to happen. Hopefully everything goes well.

We know very little about Australia but, from what Mrs. Rose told us, it must be an incredible country. This is also Mrs. Rose's first time in Sydney and she still doesn't know what she's going to do.

"I'm only staying for a few days and then I will fly back. I don't have any commitments; I just want to visit it to evaluate whether or not I want to live here one day."

According to Mrs. Rose, Australia is a country with a rich and unique nature. There are hundreds of unspoiled beaches with an abundance of corals. It's a paradise for fish and humans, who climb on wooden boards and jump into the water.

She also talked about how kangaroos carry their babies in a frontal pouch attached to their bodies and how koalas are so cute and look like stuffed animals.

"Do they also have crabs here?" Molly asks.

"Of course. There is a species of red crabs from the Christmas Islands. They migrate every year. You

can see thousands of crabs walking for days during the mating period."
That is cool! Maybe I can befriend some of them and we can exchange experiences!

 It is already dark when we leave the ship. According to Ned's calculations, the laboratory is very close to the port and we can reach it on foot. In addition, since it is after-hours, the place should already be closed, so it is a good time to enter.

 "Molly, how are we going to transport all the freed animals at once?" asks Ned.

"We can stop taxis on the street and put the animals in multiple cars."

"We don't even know how many animals are in there. And who's going to stop for a bunch of hitchhiking animals? Sorry, but I don't think it will work," I conclude.

"Do you have a better idea, Zoe?" asks Sofia.

 "Not right now, unless…"

 "Quick, hide, Mrs. Rose is approaching," says Molly, pushing our heads to the bottom of the bag. Mrs. Rose appears as fast as a comet.

"My dear, do you want to go for a walk to see the city?"

I can't believe Mrs. Rose found us.

"I'm so sorry, I can't. I have to meet my dad at the clinic."

"That's it! This is how we are going to do it. Mrs. Rose will help us!" I whisper to my friends. I can take you there, Molly if you like," says Mrs. Rose.

"No – I mean – thank you very much, but – ouch!"

"What happened? asks Ms. Rose, puzzled by Molly's little squeal of pain.

"Nothing, it must have been a mosquito biting me," says Molly, burying her face in the bag.

"Molly, she can help us," I whisper.

"How? She'll only set us back by asking a trillion questions."

"I know, but she can drive, I state.

"Of course, Mrs. Rose, thanks a lot for offering your help," Molly replies, still not completely convinced. "My dad would love to meet you."

At this very moment, a valet from a rental car company stops with a cool sportscar in front of us. Rose tips the valet and sits at the wheel.

"Great idea, Zoe, this car can hardly fit five people, where will we put everybody?" says Molly sarcastically with her face tucked in her bag again as Mrs. Rose asks her for the address.

12. Tina

We stop in front of a villa surrounded by high walls at the end of a dark street. Molly gets out of the car while Mrs. Rose calls her friends to tell them that she's finally in Australia.

"Sofia, take your phone with you and crawl underneath the door. Please, look everywhere for my father. We'll be here, following your moves with the GPS, waiting for information from you," says Molly with a firm tone, taking full leadership in the last phase of the mission.

Sofia squeezes, extends, and crawls, but she isn't able to pass underneath the door.

"Guys, I think I ate too much on the ship. I can't get through," she says, disappointed.

"And now what?" Molly puts her hands on her head.

"I don't know, but I spotted a pair of feet inside," says Sofia, still embarrassed that she ate too much and now the plan is in jeopardy because of her gluttony.

"We'll have to get inside in another way," says Ned, looking for his glasses in the bag.

"What is this?" exclaims Ned. Suddenly, we realize that Ned's bag has started working again. But what's coming out is something that we don't need at all.

"What's this? A suit, a coat and a hat? We're trying to enter a highly guarded facility and the bag is pre-paring me for a goofy party with baggy clothes?" laments Ned, less than impressed.

"Wait a second!" I jump in. "Molly could wear this outfit and pretend to be an inspector!"

"No way, I don't look like a man." Molly says, al-most offended.

"Ok, I think I know what we can do," I proclaim with bold resolve.

We glance at the car and see Mrs. Rose waving, still talking animatedly on the phone. The door of the building opens slowly, and a lady sticks her face out.

"Good evening, I'm Dr. Ned, nice to meet you," says Molly, extending her hand and entering the clinic. The receptionist also extends her hand tim-idly, a little startled.

"I'm the sales representative and I'm here to collect the supply order," Molly says with a low and coarse voice through the buttons of the suit. Ned stands on

Molly's shoulders with the hat covering the majority of his face and big sunglasses over his eyes while he lip-syncs Molly's words.

"Order? At this time in the evening?" the secretary replies, suspicious, as she picks up the phone. Meanwhile, Sofia and I slip out of Molly's pants and start roaming the clinic. The phone does not work, because Ned smartly cut the wires outside.

"I don't see anything on the agenda. I need to ask you to leave right now, because the clinic is closed. You can come back tomorrow."

"Thank you very much, young lady. We'll see you tomorrow, first thing in the morning," says Molly, shaking slightly.

Sofia and I run, well, she slithers, in the darkness, not knowing where to go. Sofia switches her phone's flashlight on and, all of a sudden, we see a pair of eyes open behind metal bars.

My God! The animals are kept captive in cells.

"Hi," I whisper. "Do you know where Mr. Jacobs is?

"I have no idea," a grumpy hippo says as he approaches the fence. "Who are you anyway? You look funny! Ask Tina, she knows everything. And don't bother me again!"

"Where do I find Tina?"

"Fourth cage on the right."

We arrive in front of a cage and see two animals sleeping on the floor.

"Tina, Tina?", I call, quietly, from outside the cage. A kangaroo turns around, slowly.

"Are you Tina?"

"Yes, I am, who are you?"

"I'm Zoe and this is Sofia. We're looking for Mr. Jacobs."

"Mr. J? He's in cell number 20."

"Thank you, we came here to release you all."

"Interesting! I was hoping that one day we'd be saved, but I thought it would be by the police, not by a foreign crab and a snake.

"Wake your friends up and get ready because we'll have to leave in a few minutes."

"Zoe, I have a disability, so I am going to have some difficulties," Tina says, pointing to a white brace on her right leg. "I can't run, but I will let Noah know."

"Tina, you also need to come," says Sofia.

"I can't even get out of the cage without Noah's help. I know that I have no way to survive outside, anyway."

"But do you want to live here forever?" I say, trying to convince her.

"I have no choice, and at least here I have food and water."

"Zoe, we have to go." Sofia pulls me with her tail.

"Tina, wake up Noah and get ready. We'll be right back."

Walking quickly down the hall, we see that some cells are full of animals. We enter cell 20 and recognize the sleeping human wrapped in bedsheets. I pinch Mr. Jacobs, who wakes up agitated while Sofia hands him the phone.

It takes him a few seconds to understand what is going on and then he calls the number on the screen.

"Molly? Where are you, kiddo?"

"Dad, I'm out here. Tell me where the keys to the cells are."

"Molly, they're in a cabinet mounted very high, it's impossible to reach."

"Tell me where it is, Daddy. We need to try."
A metal cabinet, about four meters high, is at the back of the clinic, very close to the exit. An artificial lake surrounds it, in which several poisonous snakes swim, ready to strike.

We approach it slowly, afraid of being seen. Those snakes are much longer than Sofia, with a diamond-shaped head and frightening, deep eyes. They would be able to devour us without even having to chew us.

"Maybe they're nice, like me?" whispers Sofia.

"Sofia now is not the time to find out. Look at the size of those fangs."

"Zoe, we snakes only attack to defend ourselves," says Sofia, creeping up stealthily towards the lake.

I close my eyes immediately because I am not prepared to witness this scene.

Sofia starts whistling a song and, all of a sudden, the snakes gather on one side of the lake. Wrapped around each other, they begin to calm down and immediately fall into a deep sleep.

"Zoe, climb over my head."

"Cool beans, Sofia, you made them fall asleep!"

"Yes, but let's move fast because I don't know how long their sleep will last."
At the same time, in the car, Molly and Ned, back in the bag, are waiting anxiously, while Mrs. Rose doesn't stop talking on the phone.

13. The escape

Sofia swiftly crosses the lake and creeps up to reach the top of the cabinet, until I am able, by stretching all my body in a quite uncomfortable way, to touch the keys with the tip of my claw.

After several trials, with the help of my entire body like a Tai Chi master, I finally succeed in dragging the keys towards me. Without looking down, so as not to see how far from the ground I am, I wrap my eight little legs around the keys.

I'm grateful, now, that I have so many legs. I can't believe that I used to complain about it. We climb down, careful not to wake the snakes, who are so relaxed that they snore like motorcycle engines. We go back to the cell and hand the keys to Mr. Jacobs, who storms out like a lightning bolt to go and open all the other cages.

We go to Tina's cell and spot Noah, a gray koala, preparing to leave.

"Hi Noah, we are going to help you take Tina," I tell him.

"Hi, I already insisted, but she doesn't want to leave," Noah says, shaking his head in disapproval.

 "Okay, I'll take care of it, Noah. Please run and help Sofia to free the other animals." I enter the dark cell, approach Tina and show my right claw to her.

"Look, Tina, I'm different too. I lost my little claw and, although it grew back, it's now smaller than before and will never be as developed as my left one. My movements on this side are slow and weak, but I can still do many things with it."

"But a foot problem is worse," justifies Tina, "everyone looks at me differently. I use this brace to keep my foot aligned because, unfortunately, I can't move it. My friend Noah gives me a foot massage every day, so I don't feel pain."

"Tina, I can relate to that. The animals look at you because they're curious, but after a while they get used to it. Curiosity is a reaction we have when we see something for the first time and then it becomes common."

"Zoe, I'm afraid to face the world outside," says Tina, looking at the empty cage.

"Come with me, Tina. Noah and the other animals are out there waiting for us."

Rapid footsteps approach and a loud scream startles us. The receptionist arrives, pushing Tina back into the cell. I pinch the woman's heel with all my strength as Tina limps out of the cell. Unaware of what is going on, the woman screams and backs into a corner of the cell while I lock the door with her inside.

The sound of an alarm going off suddenly fills the whole building. The only thing to do now is to get out of there as fast as humanly, or animally, possible.

"Come on Zoe, we have to get out of here," Tina says frantically, "let's go to the back exit."

Walking with difficulty, Tina and I reach the exit and see that the snakes are awake and are moving steadily in our direction.

The sound of an annoying car horn joins the deafening noise of the alarm. We suddenly spot Mrs. Rose's car already filled with all kinds of animals. Even the grumpy hippo made it with a disgusted expression on her face. It's evident that it would be impossible to fit Tina in the car.

I see a scooter parked on the sidewalk. That's it! This is exactly what we need. "Tina, lean on the wall and put your right foot with the brace on the scooter."

"Are you out of your mind, Zoe? I'm going to fall."

"No, you won't. Believe in yourself, Tina! Hold the handlebars and put all your weight on your left foot that is on the floor."

Molly, in the car with Mrs. Rose, spots us from the other side of the street and signals us to come along quickly. Suddenly, Tina and I get blinded by the powerful headlights of a car coming from the other direction.

 The blinding lights prompt Tina to forget her fears and climb quickly onto the scooter like a seasoned racer. She propels us forward with a powerful stroke of her left foot and, in a few seconds, we find ourselves behind Mrs. Rose's car.

We ride the scooter while listening to the laughter of Mrs. Rose and Mr. Jacobs through the city streets.

"Don't look back, Tina, we are being followed by a black car," I warn.

After almost 15 minutes of chase, Mrs. Rose stops in front of a police station where several policemen are waiting for us. The car that was following us had tried to turn around, but it was stopped by a police roadblock and all its passengers were brought to jail.

14. Triumph

The beach is empty, and we are all sitting together by the sea. Although it's winter in Australia, the temperature is mild, and we set up a tent just to shield ourselves from the wind.

The last few days have been exciting and tiring at the same time. This is the first time we stop to enjoy ourselves. Mrs. Rose and Mr. Jacobs play with the ball in the sand, Ned is clinging to his father, and Molly, Sofia, Noah, Tina, and I watch with admiration and pride for having succeeded in our mission.

It was just two days ago that we rescued all the animals and Mr. Jacobs has already managed to get several families to adopt them. It was exciting to see how human beings received them with such love.

"Tina, what did the scientists do to you?" I ask, curiously.

"We actually sat down once a day with Mr. J and stared at him. Sometimes we were speaking in our language, but the poor guy didn't understand us. I think it was all quite weird. Mr. J sometimes tried to sleep, but they kept waking him up with some noise on the headphones that he was forced to wear at all times."

"Zoe, those scientists were trying to turn my dad into an animal, just like they did to me," chimes in Molly, "they gave my father a potion and watched daily if his reaction to the animals was changing."

"Wow, that's crazy! I have another question, Molly. How did you convince Mrs. Rose to collect all those animals?"

"Zoe, haven't you noticed yet? Mrs. Rose loved to see all those animals coming out of the clinic."

"Seriously? So, she loves animals, too?"

"Of course, but that was not the only reason.

Mrs. Rose was on a secret mission to find out where my father was being kept hostage. But not for a moment did she think we were there for the same reason. She only realized on the last day, when I told her that my father was a veterinarian."

"So, is that's why she insisted on giving us a ride?"

"Exactly. While we were trying to get into the clinic, Mrs. Rose pretended to be talking to a friend, but in fact she was in constant contact with the police."

"So, everything she told us was a lie?" asks Sofia, disappointed.

"No Sofia, Mrs. Rose never lied, she just omitted the fact that she was an investigator and was disguised as an older lady so that she wouldn't be recognized."

"Good, because I like her very much," I say, "in fact, when are we going home? All of a sudden I have the courage to get on a plane."

"Zoe, we've decided that we're going to live here forever, and we'd like you to stay with us," Molly says, excitedly.

"I agree," says Sofia, laying on Molly's lap.

Wow, I was not expecting this! How am I going to live alone on another continent?

"Molly, I would like to stay, but I need my family."

"Don't worry Zoe, everything is already planned." Says Ned showing me an airplane timetable.

"What do you mean by 'everything' is already planned, Ned?"

"Well, tomorrow, your family will be arriving with a friend of my dad, says Molly. We'll pick them up at the airport in the morning.

...

Mom runs out of the cage with my brothers, Suzy, Jenny, and her daughter. Everyone stumbles over each other, not knowing where to run. Jenny sees her husband for the first time in a while and starts crying tears of joy.

Mom and my brothers jump on top of me.

We've been here for two months now and we live on a paradisiacal beach.

Our house is much cozier than the old one, and Ned's family lives in a futuristic, bamboo house underneath a palm tree.

Sofia has started to sing daily, attracting other snakes. She is confident that she will soon lay her eggs.

 Mr. Jacobs married Mrs. Rose, who is no longer wearing a disguise and they have adopted Tina and Noah.

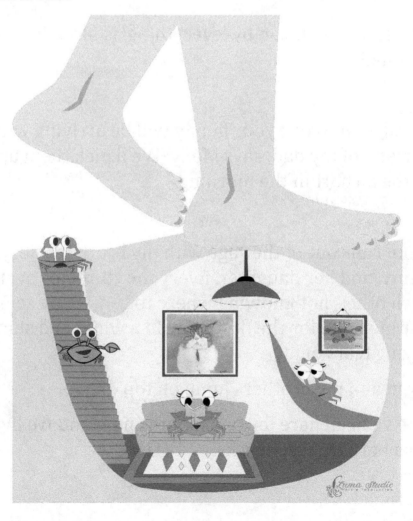

Paco asked for Suzy's hand and she accepted.

Molly is scheduling a march to create awareness for the preservation of nature and has already managed to get several humans to participate.

Tina has physical therapy sessions daily and is already having good results. In the meantime, she strolls all over town with her brand-new electric scooter.

Juan got quieter. He spends his time watching birds and has started writing romantic songs.

Mom opened a nursery and my house is always full of baby crabs.

My current hobby is climbing the palm trees, while Sofia follows and rescues me, if needed. My fear of heights is, now, under control.

I've made friends with several cool crabs and nowadays I lead the excursions on the neighboring beaches.

My days are beautiful, and I have never been happier in my life!

CPSIA information can be obtained
at www.ICGtesting.com
Printed in the USA
LVHW051142291220
675197LV00003B/583